Love Is Treason

Nathaniel Apheyso

Dreamland Publishing
Lagos

© 2012 Nathaniel Apheyso

All rights reserved. No part of this publication may be reproduced, stored in retrieved system or transmitted in any form or by any means – electronic, mechanical, photocopying or otherwise – without the prior permission of the copyright owner.

ISBN 978-978-912-438-1

Nathaniel Apheyso

Acknowledgement

I wish to express my deep appreciation to a number of people who assisted me during the writing of this book. My profound gratitude goes to Emmanuel Adewale Stephen, Samuel Oriloye Joseph, Thadeaous Oyinieh Joseph, John Brown Adegunsoye and my entire family.

Dedication

To all those the victims of injustice and oppression.

CHARACTERS

HEALER	Mitota
OGBAJI	King of Egbetua
IREYAN	Princess of Egbetua
EREMASE	King of Udurebo
AMUME	Eremase's Wife
OMORE	Princess of Udurebo
AFWONE	Omore's lover
MAHKE	Omore's friend
OMOYE	Omore's maid
OKUKU	Soothsayer
IGBE	Eremase's gardener
ITOTE	Igbe's wife

AMINEBUE Igbe's daughter

ASEME
OVOAME Citizens of Udurebo

OYASE

AGBOTO

CHIEFS,ELDERS,MAIDENS,BODYGUARDS, TOWNSPEOPLE

SETTING: UDUREBO KINGDOM

Prologue

There are flashes of light on stage every now and then accompanied by beating of musical instrument as a song is being sung along with humming in the background, all in sorrowful manner.

VOICE:

Koso nogbikhemo sagbo samine nosegbereooo…
Humanity has come into the world to toil and labour
Koso nogbikhemo sagbo samine nosegbereooo…
Humanity has come into the world to toil and labour
Koso nogbikhemo sagbo samine nosegbereeeee…
Humanity has come into the world to toil and labour
Koso nogbikhemo sagbo samine nosegbereooo…
Humanity has come into the world to toil and labour

CHORUS:

Ingme bagbooo…
Matters of life
Koko kenooo…
They are proverbial
Ingme bagbooo…
Matters of life
Koko kenooo…
They are proverbial
Ingme bagbooo…
Matters of life
Koko kenooo…
They are proverbial
Koso nogbikhemo sagbo samine
nosegbereooo…
*Humanity has come into the world to toil and
labour*
Koso nogbikhemo sagbo samine
nosegbereooo…
*Humanity has come into the world to toil and
labour*
Koso nogbikhemo sagbo samine
nosegbereeeee…
*Humanity has come into the world to toil and
labour*
Koso nogbikhemo sagbo samine
nosegbereooo…

Humanity has come into the world to toil and labour

CHORUS:

Ingme bagbooo…
Matters of life
Koko kenooo…
They are proverbial

Ingme bagbooo…
Matters of life
Koko kenooo…
They are proverbial
Ingme bagbooo…
Matters of life
Koko kenooo…
They are proverbial

(Song gradually fades away while humming continues in the background. Light focuses on stage showing a man whose hands are tied to the back standing to address the audience)

AFWONE:

The axe is waiting by my neck in the hand of my executioner as I make my last speech. Did you ask why? (*He pauses*) The kingdom of Udurebo has charged me with treason. Treason for what? For the fact that … (*He turns and looks away from the audience.*) Well, sorry that, I am not permitted to say. Life has been quite unfair to me. The greed of humanity has led me to where I am now. I can't tell you my story because I'd soon be dead. (*He pauses again.*) Hopefully, someday, somebody somewhere will tell my story. They say it is my destiny. It may or may not be. The fact that a man sets up a fire does not mean it cannot consume him (*He turns to look away from the audience.*) Sorry, my time is up, I must now face the axe. (*He goes behind a log standing erect, bending over it with his hand tied to his back. Executioner approaches raising his axe up. Black out. The song picks up again with humming and the sorrowful playing of a musical instrument.*)

VOICE:

Koso nogbikhemo sagbo samine
nosegbereooo…
Humanity has come into the world to toil and
labour
Koso nogbikhemo sagbo samine
nosegbereooo…
Humanity has come into the world to toil and
labour
Koso nogbikhemo sagbo samine
nosegbereeeee…
Humanity has come into the world to toil and
labour
Koso nogbikhemo sagbo samine
nosegbereooo…
Humanity has come into the world to toil and
labour

CHORUS:

Ingme bagbooo…
Matters of life

Koko kenooo…
They are proverbial
Ingme bagbooo…
Matters of life
Koko kenooo…

They are proverbial
Ingme bagbooo…
Matters of life
Koko kenooo…
They are proverbial
Koso nogbikhemo sagbo samine nosegbereooo…
Humanity has come into the world to toil and labour
Koso nogbikhemo sagbo samine nosegbereooo…
Humanity has come into the world to toil and labour
Koso nogbikhemo sagbo samine nosegbereeeee…
Humanity has come into the world to toil and labour
Koso nogbikhemo sagbo samine nosegbereooo…
Humanity has come into the world to toil and labour
(Beating and humming gradually fades away.)

Nathaniel Apheyso

Act One Scene One

Stage opens somewhere in the forest of Ogbeani. Enter an aged woman on stage, a white wrapper tied above her breast and a girdle above her waist with some leaves in her hand. Night noise is being heard as she stops to examine the bunch in her hand. The stage is poorly lit.

HEALER:

(*She looks up to face the audience*) It is always better to get these leaves after sunset because that is when you get the best out of them for use. Those who know nothing about them, consider them common and ordinary leaves. (*She pauses*) It is ignorance that makes a child refer to medicine as mere vegetables. Leaves and roots never failed our ancestors, neither would they fail us. In certain instances, though, they are not of much use when it is linked with a disease of the mind, having to do with love.

(*She pauses*) I am a healer of the disease associated with the mind and know well from countless experiences that matters of love should not be imposed on the young, especially women of this generation and perhaps beyond. Love in the heart of a woman is stronger than intoxicating liquor and is as deep as the ocean. If you dare provoke this natural feeling, you would have exhumed a monster out of an abyss. (*She pauses*) Parents, I particularly appeal to you to watch and learn from the error of our great grand fathers. To begin, let us start with my recent patient, Princess Ireyan. (*Enters a maiden to deliver a message*)

FIRST MAIDEN:

Iyanme (*She kneels slightly in respectful greeting*) The king of Egbetua, King Ogbaji, has just arrived. He demands to speak with you.

HEALER:

Tell him I would be with him in a moment.

FIRST MAIDEN:

Very well, Iyanme. (*She kneels slightly and exits*)

HEALER:

(*She turns to face the audience*) I was saying let's see what we can learn from the case of Princess Ireyan before that interruption. The king of Egbetua's arrival is just on time. Now our play can begin as you watch events unfold before your eyes (*She exits*)

Act One Scene Two

Enter King Ogbaji on stage followed by first chief and three body guards. The king and his chief both take their seat while the bodyguards stand around them. Second maiden enters with an insane lady, making her sit on the bare floor some distance away, while she sits on a seat close by her. The king and chief shake their heads in despair. First maiden enters.

FIRST MAIDEN:

(*Kneeling slightly in greeting*) Your Highness, Iyanme has been informed of your arrival. She would be with you in a short while. (*She takes a bow and exit. At the other side of the stage, second maiden smacks insane lady over some misdeed*)

IREYAN:

Ahaa! Why beat me for a fault that is not mine? She asked me to keep the baby fire warm, so I decided to set the child on fire.

SECOND MAIDEN:

Shut up your dirty mouth or else I'd shut it up for you!

IREYAN:

Yes of course I would do that after the truth has been told the whole world. They must hear my own side of the story.

SECOND MAIDEN:

See who's talking. What does a mad girl like you know?

IREYAN:

You are wrong; I am not a girl but rather a married woman. My husband traveled on a journey, though some people think he is taking long in coming. I am sure he is missing my warm embrace. He would return to my arms again, so I won't lose hope. People say a foreign woman has cast a spell on him causing him to forget home.

The spell of a foreign land may be powerful but my spells are even stronger. For the spell of my bosom would bring him back home. She may cast lustful spell, but I, too, am a witch and the spell I cast on him is true love. When he returns to me then will all know that my spells are stronger. (*There are tears in her eyes*) I know he would return to be my beloved husband again, so I would not despair. Though there are tears in my eyes but I would not cry. I'd hold them back and prove myself strong (*She begins to cry*) I can hold it no longer. Please, let me cry and unburden my heart. (*She weeps even more*)

SECOND MAIDEN:

Silent you stupid brat! I have tolerated your nuisance long enough but this crying of yours is choking me to death. (*She makes a whip out of rag close by and begins to flog her with it causing her to cry even more. Her crying gradually fades. Healer enters on stage at the other end to join King Ogbaji and his chief*).

HEALER:

Your Highness, king of Egbetua, you are welcome to the land of Ogbeani!

OGBAJI:

May the gods of my land and of Ogbeani grant you success in your entire endeavor, Mitota. I have come in response to your urgent request.

FIRST CHIEF:

We had to leave Egbatua in the evening to arrive Ogbeani by night.

HEALER:

I regret whatever inconveniences my call must have cost you Your Highness. (*She pauses*) Our people say that a crying eye still maintains its vision. I called you in connection with your daughter. (*Pointing toward her, she helps herself with a seat*) I have exhausted all remedies without any sign of improvement. A once fruitful tree does not suddenly wither off without a serious cause.

(*She pauses*) When one is sick, getting the desired cure depends on knowing the root cause of the very illness. Tell me, what is it that led to her present condition?

OGBAJI:

(*Silent for a while*) Hmmm! Mitota you and I have come a long way, even from our childhood. I'd rather not want to talk about it.

HEALER:

Granting your wish Your Highness is as easy as the way the eye lashes blink, except that the situation right now is gradually draining off the fluid of life from your daughter. Believe me Your Highness; the woman that sells tobacco snuff sees different palms of people.

OGBAJI:

I would understand if you want a raise of your fee over my daughter's illness.

HEALER:

You should have known me better, Your Highness, that I fear not to say whatever is on my mind. Even the offer of a treasure house would not lead us anywhere, except we deal with the issue from the root source. (*She pauses*) Your Highness, the king, I need to really know the events that led to your daughter's present state.

OGBAJI:

That is an ugly tale I do not wish to tell; the subject irritates me.

HEALER:

Does it still annoy His Highness?

OGBAJI:

I would no longer want to continue with this conversation.

HEALER:

As it pleases His Highness.

FIRST CHIEF:

(*Clears his throat*) Forgive me, Your Highness, should I sound rude. Is it not wise to pay heed to the voice of reason rather than insist on matters the way they are? Your Highness, it is the very well being of the princess of Egbetua that we are talking about here. (*Pauses*) When does a she-bear ever stop caring for her cubs? If the Odafe is insistent, then so be it. But I shall speak, Your Highness, even if I incur your wrath. When a tree full of green leaves suddenly withers off, it does certainly have a cause. (*Pauses*) The princess went against His Highness' wish. She stooped low beyond her class, falling in love with a mere slave; she was head strong; and considering the fact that she is an only child. The princess turned down all eligible suitors. It is unheard of and unacceptable for a slave to preside over the kingdom of Egbetua.

On the side lines, enemies and rivals watch with interest wanting to take advantage of the situation.

To remedy it, the king did what was thought to be fair and wise by selling this slave in question to a faraway land, where the princess will never set her eyes on him again. Initially, everyone thought that she would get over the issue overtime. But as it turns out, her reaction became abnormal getting worse by each day until it became a chronic illness of the mind. It is for fear of her situation getting out of hand that informed her being brought to you. This is the whole truth of the matter if at all it could be of any use to you Mitota.

HEALER:

Hmmm! I can now discern why the nose is embittered with the mouth. (*Pause*) This very matter is tingling to the ears. Now that the cause has been identified, we can now tackle it.

FIRST CHIEF:

You mean we can have hope for her recovery?

HEALER:

The bedbug tells its children that whatever gets hot must cool down. We can have a cure to the princess' illness if His highness so wishes.

FIRST CHIEF:

What sort of talk is that? One cannot have a drum in his hut yet beat the drum with his stomach, can he?

HEALER:

Your Highness, I would wait until you speak.

OGBAJI:

What would you have me do to convince you that I want a cure for my daughter? All you need do is ask.

HEALER:

The shell of a palm fruit is hard; still a monkey would swallow it if only it would ease the tension in its stomach.

FIRST CHIEF:

Why do you keep speaking in riddle?. Break the coconut, so that the water can spill for the eyes to see.

OGBAJI:

Our people say that the stubborn child is not the fault of the male organ. Mitota, you know she is my only child and my only hope of a male heir.

HEALER:

In truth, Your Highness, a bad child has his or her own usefulness. (*Pauses*) There is a thin thread between life and death. I can only wonder if one would wait for the right time to pull the string.

FIRST CHIEF:

You conceal too much wordings in your riddle woman. Spill the coconut water for the king to sip from.

HEALER:

All we need to heal the princess is at our disposal. But what is missing for now is the motivation to make them work.

FIRST CHIEF:
Can't you ever speak for once without a coded tongue? I hate…

HEALER:
The slave you sold away is the missing link to this very matter.

OGBAJI:
I am aware that you are trying to make a point which I am yet to comprehend. So I'd suggest you smash the calabash to unveil what is hidden from the eyes.

HEALER:
As a healer I have the medication to heal the princess, but to succeed we need a definite motivation. It may be hard to accept certain facts Your Highness. We need the slave boy around her if we will ever hope for a healing.

OGBAJI:

(*Springing up in anger*) I can see that my enemies are every step ahead of me. What I never thought was that they could get to you of all people. (*Pauses*) A child who is carried on the shoulder does not know how far the journey is.

HEALER:

Your Highness, it is good that you desire a cure for your ailing child but you seem to have forgotten that one who wants to eat and drink from the coconut must give up comfort to remove its outer shell. (*She pauses*) With utmost sincerity, I sympathize with His Highness' situation on this matter. What one does not feel one cannot claim to know. The crown is a symbol of royalty and one cannot but agree that royalty should be jealously guarded. (*Pauses*) If I am correct, the princess is the king's only source of producing a legitimate heir.

So why do we have to put the fattest bull on the altar of sacrifice for the prestige of a mere dog? (*She sighs and pauses*) Caution oh king, caution! We must tread this very path cautiously; otherwise this little fire we see may consume great men of honor. You may wonder what I mean. But for a while, pay attention and see for yourself.

Exeunt

Act Two Scene One

Somewhere, on the street of Udurebo Enter two maidens of royal lineage on stage from the right, walking toward the left hand side of stage, then stop to talk ; one of them is more beaded than the other. They are followed behind by three maids and a bodyguard.

OMORE:

I wish I could go about freely in the kingdom of Udurebo without being followed by maids and bodyguards.

MAHKE:

What kind of wish is that? You seem to have forgotten that you are the lone princess and heir to the throne.

OMORE:

That is the very reason I hate royalty, I mean the burden of royalty, such as mine. I'd love to be a private person, being able to walk the streets of Udurebo without anyone looking over my shoulder, not catching the attention of the crowd. I love to relate with every citizen freely and be treated like every normal person on a bush path.

MAHKE:

Though you are my friend, Omore, you never cease to amaze me.(*Clapping her hands, she pause and walked away from the rest and then returned to join them*) You call royalty a burden or what did you say? For me I've only had a little from enough. Wait until one of those princes from our neighboring kingdom comes to my parent to ask for my hand in marriage, and then you'd discover how much I cherish it. As for me, I love royalty, especially the glamour that goes with it (*She gestures, showing off her beauty*) I love royalty along with its glamour. (*She says sarcastically*)

OMORE:

That is you, not me. Just take a look at these maids. (*Pointing at them*) Don't you think they deserve better treatment than they are given?

After all, they are humans like us. And look at that one. (*Pointing to the bodyguard*) Don't you think he would have better things to do with his life than following a mere woman like me around?

MAHKE:

Oh Stop it Omore! Your words irritate me. I have tolerated you enough this time. How dare you bring the throne as far as to the dust? You seem to be forgetting whose daughter you are. May I remind you that you are the legitimate heir to the throne of Udurebo.

OMORE:

Really! Hmm,…I seem to have forgotten that my dear friend.(*sounding sarcastically and then pause*)Look here *ocharime!*, lay pride by the dust and put on humility but for a while Mahke. Open your eyes and see the beautiful world around you. Royalty has played god for too long than it deserves. (*Suddenly they begin to hear drum and metallic instrument, accompanied by a flutist playing out his rhythm, gradually gathering momentum*)

MAHKE:

I can see you are enjoying the musical rhythm coming from the distance.

OMORE:

I'd certainly want to reach the source of this musical delight, after all today is Itakpo Festival. (*She charges forward and then turn to face others in excitement*) My mother says good music heals one's soul during troubled times. Come on!(*Beckoning on them*) Lets go and catch some fun.

MAHKE:

You detest royalty despite your royal root and rather envy commoners, wishing to have a root among them yet you enjoy the very product that springs from royalty. Hmmmn hmmmn. Omore, you just won't stop surprising me.

OMORE:

Say what you so wish, after all, you own your mouth. But certainly

I'd not give you the pleasure of making me feel guilty. Come on, my naughty friend, enough talking. Let us go and receive some musical healing for our souls. (*She run off stage through the opposite direction, Mahke and the maids keep up the chase followed by bodyguard*)

Exeunt

Act Two Scene Two

Stage opens in the palace of Udurebo Enter King Eremase and sits on his throne, followed by his chiefs. Two bodyguards stand on both side of the king. Chiefs greet the king and then remain standing as they speak.

EREMASE:

How has matters fared today in the land of Udurebo?

FIRST CHIEF:

Your Highness, everything went well. The people of Udurebo were all in the spirit of festivity.*(He speaks enthusiastically, throwing his body, from side to side)*

SECOND CHIEF

(He claps his hands in excitement) Our young men have grown from boys to men. Just as past generations have handed over to us, we are equally handing over to them the legacy in our possession.

EREMASE:

May our ancestor bathe them with the depth of our rich cultural heritage and as well fill them with the wisdom of our deities.*(He seats down after speaking and others joined him)*

ALL CHIEFS:

Iseeeh!

SECOND CHIEF:

Your Highness, there were lots of other side attractions that added to the festivity.

FIRST CHIEF:

There were lots of food and drinks showing the dept of our wealth. But I think the music caught my attention the most. The musicians held all spectators spell bound, that I wish I were ten years younger your highness.

THIRD CHIEF:

For me, your Highness, the main attraction was the pretty young maidens. (*He jump to his feet, describing an imaginary maidens curves with both hands*) Truthfully, just as he said, they held me spell bound(*sits down*) I really wish I were younger.

FIRST CHIEF:

Don't tell me you are considering taking an eight wife at this time of your old age.

THIRD CHIEF:

You amaze me my friend. What else would an old man like me do with his time? Or do you expect me to be still working my heart out after Uvose the god of fertility has blessed me so much?

SECOND CHIEF:

If you are still so excited about young maidens, I would not be surprised if you walk in here one of these days bent half your height for over working your aging muscles.

THIRD CHIEF:

At my age, I am still as strong as a lion, *(He rise to show off his physic)* yes still very active than your first son.

SECOND CHIEF:

Satisfy your appetite as you so desire but only one thing: make sure you keep your lustful eyes away from the princess.

THIRD CHIEF:

(Still standing) That the cat has kept its calm does not mean the rat should overstep its boundary. On the other hand, if the Odafe consider me honorable enough, then it's an offer I'd dare not reject. *(Sits down)*

FIRST CHIEF:

If young men could wish and hope, what harm is there if an old man dreams mere dreams. (*All in the palace laugh in amusement except the guards*)

EREMASE:

It gladdens my heart to know that this year's Itakpo festivity has been successful. May Ememah be praised and receive due dignity for his watchful eyes over Udurebo.

ALL CHIEFS:

Isseeeeh!

SECOND CHIEF:

That reminds me, Your Highness. Agbeda, the merchant asked me to inform you that he has a few slaves he thinks would interest you.

FIRST CHIEF:

We shall see to that when the time comes. Less I forget your highness, today is the day we set aside to attend to the sharing of late Ubuoro"s family land dispute. If you can remember.

EREMASE:

Hmmm.. May the Ememah bless your memory for not losing sight of such an important issue; else it would have been embarrassing to us all.

THIRD CHIEF:

Actually I was just about mentioning it to you your highness if not that I opted to pause before speaking.

EREMASE:

I sure do understand, after all, it has always been like that with you.(*He turn to face first chief*)I need you all to live at once to attend to that issue. I'd be here waiting until you bring me back words on how matters were resolve.

FIRST CHIEF:

Very well your highness. We shall attend to these matters at once just as you've directed (*He takes a bow and then turn to exit. Other chiefs did the same following after him*)

EREMASE:

(*He pause to think and then soliloquize*) Hmm…

The very thought of death frightens one. Imagine, Ubuoro my friend has suddenly become of late memory. Who knows whose turn it could be next? I just hope these uneasy feeling am having has got no hands with the cruel touch of death.(*He rise from his throne and begin to exit*) I must send for Okuku at once to ensure that the shadow of evil intent does not creep in on us like birth pangs.

Exeunt

Act Two Scene Three

Behind the palace, somewhere in the princess quarters. Enter Omore on stage accompanied by three maids following her behind.

OMORE:

You can all now go. I think I need some privacy for myself. On a second thought, you!(*Pointing to one of the maidens*) stay with me while the rest of you can go. (*Maid points herself as if not sure*) Come here! Come sit with me. (*Omore sits down*) What is that your name again?

OMOYE:

Omoye, my princess. (*Kneeling slightly respectfully*)

OMORE:

Ah! You see, our names even sound alike. Come, take a sit beside me.

OMOYE:

No my princess, our tradition does not permit me to do so. Besides, His Highness and the queen would not be pleased with such undue familiarity.

OMORE:

Oh! Yes, that is the more reason I am choosing you as my friend and confidant. I've always liked you since the first day I saw you.

OMOYE:

I cannot do that my princess. Please, I beg of you.

OMORE:

Do you want to annoy me Omoye?

OMOYE:

No my princess, I wouldn't dare to do such a thing.

OMORE:

Please, I need you to be my friend, even if it means

I have to beg because for sure I can't force you. I'd stay on my kneels until you say yes. (*She kneels down while speaking*)

OMOYE:

Ah! My princess, please, pleases, please. What are you doing (*She looks left and right*) I could get into serious trouble by this humble act of yours. (*She helps her up*) Get up please! True, you can't force your friendship on me, but you don't have to beg either.

OMORE:

Is that your own way of saying yes to my request?

OMOYE:

I'm all yours my princess, body and soul, so long it will please you.

OMORE:

Oh thank you so much for accepting me. (*She hugs her in excitement*) Thank you very much.

OMOYE:

But why do you need me for a friend, when you already have Mahke?

OMORE:

Mahke! She is too worldly and imposing for my liking. I need a friend who understands and feels what I feel. Do you think I don't see? I can see the expression of understanding in your eyes even without saying a word. It is obvious you are older than me and I can use some good advice of an old sincere friend.

OMOYE:

I'd try, my princess. I'd try.

OMORE:

No, don't call me princess, call me by my name. A true friend calls one by name. Whenever you do that, it will be music to my ears. Do you understand?

OMOYE:

As you wish my princess,(*Omore gave her hard stare*) Oh sorry, Omore. (*One of the maids comes in*)

FIRST MAID:

My princess, your mother the Queen, is looking for you. (*She bows and exit, followed immediately by Omoye*)

AMUME:

Where is my princess? (*Queens's voice is heard from the distance before coming on stage*) Ah! There you are. My child, the very pupil of my eyes.(*She stretches her arms out to her for an embrace but she ignores her mother*)

OMORE:

Mother! (*She rises and walk away from her*) You pamper me too much for my liking that I feel as if I were a child.

AMUME:

And what more are you? My child of course you are, even now and after you become married and bear me children.

My child, you will always be my baby. Come, come my child. (*She sits down and have her come sits on her lap*) I hope you enjoyed your walk through the kingdom of Udurebo?

OMORE:
Very well mother. You know it's always brings me much pleasure.

AMUME:
I'm glad that you chose today of all days to walk through Udurebo. Certainly many eyes must have fed on your beautiful frame and delicate skin. Hopefully, several suitors will soon start coming to show their interest. (*She gets up out of irritation, walking away from her*)

OMORE:
Mother!

AMUME:
Yes! You must be prepared to pick the very best of them, since that one is going to become the next king of Udurebo.

OMORE:

Oh mother! Must you always bring this very subject up every time you have the slightest opportunity?

AMUME:

Yes!

OMORE:

But why must that be?

AMUME:

Because I was exactly in your kind of situation when I married your father. Our tradition forbids him from marrying any other wife alongside me. But you, the oracle says will bear us many children. I can't wait to carry them in my arms, nurture and care for them. May the spirit of Uvose the god of fertility fill your womb with many children. (*She rises to her feet*) Lest I forget, your father longs to see you. (*The Queen exit and Omore after making some irritating gesture followed after her*)

AMUME:
I'd tell your father, the king that you'd be in his presence in a short while (*Her voice echoes even after leaving the stage*)

Exeunt

Act Two Scene Four

King Eremase enters the palace dressed casually with a wrapper tied about his waist, bare-chested, pacing about.

EREMASE:

(*Soliloquizing*) When the skies are blue our fathers say it is a sign that a good day lies ahead, but when fire red, that it is a bad omen. The skies of Udurebo are blue for a little while and then suddenly fire red. (*Pauses*) My staff has dropped from my hand three times today. As far as I can guess, it is a bad omen. Up till this very moment, all has been going well in the land of Udurebo. (*Pauses*) Could it be that something bad has happened that is yet to come to light or is about to occur? I can't seem to place my finger on it. The Itakpo festival is a period when everyone within the kingdom is expected to keep peace.

I do hope our enemies are not planning to sneak in on us. Or could it be that someone within Udurebo has committed a sacrilege? The more I wonder, the more anxious I become. Every time I have such strong premonition, an eventuality always occurs. Hmmm… I must consult Okuku to get to the root of this matter by sorting the mind of the oracle because an empty sack does not stand upright. (*He returns to sit on his throne. Shortly, Omore enters*)

OMORE:
Good evening Your Majesty, the Odafe.
(*She kneels before her father*)

EREMASE:
Good evening my beloved princess. (*He places his staff on her in approval*)

OMORE:
The queen, my mother, said you long to see my face. (*She rises to sit adjacent him*)

EREMASE:

Quite true. You know that feasting my eyes on your beauty brings me much satisfaction.

OMORE:

Oh father! There you go again; teasing me has always been your habit that I can hardly tell when your words are genuine or not.

EREMASE:

My child, whenever I speak to you , I do so in truth, though it is also meant to make you smile for my delight. Even Uvose the god of fertility can testify to this fact, that your beauty is so enchanting like no other in Udurebo.

OMORE:

But today, as I walked round the kingdom, I met and saw several young ladies much prettier than I am.

ERAMASE:

Your eyes deceived you my princess. What you see in the mirror is not what you look. I, your father, your foremost admirer, is your true mirror. A mirror could be deceitful but your father would never be.

OMORE:

Who am I to doubt the words of His Majesty? If His Highness thinks his daughter is beautiful, then she most certainly is elegantly adorable.

EREMASE:

I like the sound of that. And make sure no one else convinces you otherwise. (*They both begin to laugh*) Your mother told me you went walking through Udurebo all day.

OMORE:

Yes, Your Highness. It was a lovely experience.

EREMASE:

When a crocodile goes on an expedition, a few things must have caught his attention along the way. So tell me, what it is that caught your interest.

OMORE:

Countless things, father. Things most royalties don't find amusing.*(She rise and pace about, gesturing as she speaks, pouring out her heart)* Children singing and dancing to the applause of their mates on the streets of Udurebo. Playful young men and women of my age on their way to the stream, teasing and jeering. The fun of splashing water while they take a dip in the river. Watching my mates carrying pots of water, singing melodiously in their group as they return home. The gossips, whispering and teasing were my favorite part of the adventure. Oh father! I wish I could live like every normal person in Udurebo, without bodyguards, being followed around by maidens or given preferential treatments in whatsoever I do.

EREMASE:

Hmm…Were there no other things that caught your attention?

OMORE:

These things caught my attention the most father because they are things I may never be privileged to enjoy like these commoners.

EREMASE:

You make it sound as if royalty is a burden.

OMORE:

Royalty denies me the right of childhood,(*Pacing about*) like every other normal child in Udurebo, shutting me out from seeing the world around me.

EREMASE:

(*Pauses*) Young you may be, but you speak with the wisdom of the aged. The rhythm of your words is like sweet lyrics to my ears.

OMORE:

(*Excitedly*) That reminds me father. I saw a flute playing slave, whose play delighted my soul.

I've never seen anyone play like him. This slave is up for sale. I beg of you Your Majesty, buy him for my sake.

EREMASE:

If this flute- playing slave impresses you so much, then I have no choice but to buy him.

OMORE:

Oh thank you father. (*She rises to embrace him in gratitude, excitedly*)

EREMASE:

Who is the owner of this very slave?

OMORE:

Agbeda the merchant Your Highness

EREMASE:

Ah! I can now see why he had earlier sent words to me. By this time tomorrow that slave would be at your beck and call.

OMOYE:

Oh father thank you so much. (*She hugs the king*) I wish all the fathers in Udurebo were as lovely as mine. (*She runs off stage in sheer excitement*)

Exeunt

Act Three Scene One

King Eremase enters the palace to sit. Chiefs come in to sit as well.

EREMASE:

When a man looks across his shoulder and sees his kinsmen standing behind him, he feels bold to speak to the enemies by the gate. I am glad to have you with me as I await the coming of Okuku.

FIRST CHIEF:

No grain of sand stands alone to withstand the test of time Your Highness. However, we consider ourselves honored to be bestowed with such rare privilege.

SECOND CHIEF:

The very beauty of a man's laughter lies in the companionship the teeth enjoy. One does not appreciate this fact until one of them is missing.

THIRD CHIEF:

The cluster of stars high above in the skies is a delight to the naked eyes, yet is a lesson from the inanimate to the animate. We all certainly need one another to successfully weather through life challenges, else make grave errors that could cost us dearly.

EREMASE:

You've all spoken in wisdom. Our people say a problem shared is a problem solved. (*Pauses*) A sudden fear has overwhelmed me these few days. But what it is I cannot tell. That is why I have sent for Okuku to peer into the wisdom of the wise ones to reveal what it really is.

THIRD CHIEF:

A wise gesture can never be under valued Your Highness. Your actions are wise and may the spirit of the Supreme Being continue to guide you.

SECOND CHIEF:

When Okuku says he would be right behind you, even just at a blink of an eye he is already at your door post waiting on you. I'm certain he would be here soon. (*They begin to hear foot falls with clashing metals tied to his feet*) I said it Your Highness, he is already here. (*Okuku enters with a short skirt covering his waist to the thigh and a long stick in his right hand, having a small bag hanging on his left shoulder. He spits to three directions as he comes into the palace*)

OKUKU:

I spit on you all. I curse and banish you. And you and even you that lay in wait on my path. May you flee as the shadows of darkness flee from the imminent presence of light. Where the light resides darkness seeks no refuge. His Royal Highness, king of Udurebo, to you I pay homage along with you chiefs. (*He sits on the bare floor*)

EREMASE:

Okuku, the lion of our dark jungle, you are welcome. May our ancestors honor you the way you've honored my call.

ALL CHIEFS:

Iseeeh! (*Okuku drops his small bag on the floor and brings out a piece of chalk and begins to write on the floor*)

EREMASE:

Yesterday I tripped three times and I know it's a bad omen. What it is, I need to know.

OKUKU:

Hmmm... (*Reciting incantations*) The oracle unravels what is hidden. Ememah the all knowing is wise Your Highness. What the oracle reveals is about your daughter.

EREMASE:

What did the oracle say about my daughter? (*Eagerly*) That she is about to befallen by evil?

OKUKU:

Your daughter the lone princess of Udurebo. (*Pauses*) Princess Omore finds favour with Ememah.

ALL CHIEFS:

May Ememah be praised! May he be praised! Iseeh. May he be praised.

OKUKU:

Omore is a special child your highness and must be treated accordingly. She may be a female child but the oracle says she will bring Udurebo fame and fortune than Udurebo had ever known. Her achievements will be far greater than any male king Udurebo had ever known. Her womb is filled with plenty of children. (*Pauses*) Sadly, the light she radiates suddenly will be extinguished.

ALL IN PALACE:

May Ememah forbid such evil!

OKUKU:

Yes, may he forbid! (*Pauses*) Your Highness, Omore is a rare child. What she wants she gets. Ememah says she must not be provoked else Udurebo will be engulfed by fire.

Our forefathers say zeal without knowledge is a runaway horse. Caution! Caution! Caution, I say to you oh *Odafe* of our land. Some people are wise, others are otherwise. May you be wise Your Highness. May you be wise!

EREMASE:

What in particular does the gods want me to do regarding her?

OKUKU:

The oracle has said it all, Your Highness, that there is nothing more to be said. Caution! Caution! Caution I say, else you may be raking ember into your bosom without realizing it. (*He picks up his small bag and placed it on his left shoulder and rise to exit. As he walks, the sound of clashing metals tied to his legs filled the air gradually fading away*) Those who fail to pursue their aspiration will end up becoming destitute. He who sows the seed of vengeance is sure to come in with a basket full of bloody grapes. So caution! Caution! Caution I say o leaders of Udurebo.

Caution! Caution! Caution! Caution I say.(*His voice gradually fade into the distance*)

Exeunt

Act Three Scene Two

Somewhere in the forest of Udurebo. Princess Omore, Omoye and Afwone come on stage. Omore sits at the middle of the stage, Omoye a little to her left, while Afwone sits on a log by the extreme right, playing on his flute melodically to the ladies' delight. He is bare-chested with a skirt on his waist a little above his kneels as he plays on for a while.

OMOYE:

(*She walks towards Omore, placing her hand on her shoulder*) I think it's time we start heading toward Udurebo before darkness suddenly creeps in on us.

OMORE:

Omoye, why are you in such a hurry? I'm just beginning to enjoy myself.

OMOYE:

I am equally enjoying myself, my princess. But should one enjoy a climb so much that he now climbs the tree beyond the leaf? No, my princess, as that will amount to nothing but disaster.

OMORE:

You insist too much and stretch your argument to establish your point Omoye. In any case, I see the truthfulness of your point.

OMOYE:

I feel honored, my princess. More importantly, it is for your safety and well being that I speak.

OMORE:

Afwone that will be enough for now. It's getting late, we should start heading toward the palace before darkness falls.

AFWONE:

Very well, my princess.

OMORE:

I thought I warned you not to address me in the ways of royalty, yet you persist.

AFWONE:

I am sorry, my princess, I mean not to offend you. It's just that…

OMORE:

It's just that what, Afwone? Why are you determined to hurt a sore I am nursing?

AFWONE:

Please forgive me, my princess. I'd never provoke your annoyance at will, kindly forgive me. (*He kneels down apologetically*)

OMORE:

(*She rushes to raise him up*) Please rise to your feet and keep your manly honor.

AFWONE:

May Ememah honor you the way you've honored me, my princess. May he replenish the very source of your magnanimity!

OMOYE:

Iseeeh! May he replenish it abundantly!

OMORE:

Afwone, you may go ahead of us. (*He nods and exits*)

OMOYE:

(*Laughing and clapping her hands*) Nhmmm...I hope I didn't miss any thing?

OMORE:

Why do you mock me in laughter, Omoye?

OMOYE:

Don't you think the word mockery is too strong?

OMORE:

I'd pretend I didn't hear that. (*Pause*) It appears to me that you are taking our friendship for granted as an excuse to talk back at me. However, even if it's not, I must say it was appropriate for the circumstances.

OMOYE:

I wouldn't dare, my princess.

OMORE:

So how come you are now questioning my judgment?

OMOYE:

Does that mean that the princess doubts my loyalty to her?

OMORE:

In no way my friend. Still I really want to know the motive behind your amusement.

OMOYE:

Despite the dept of the ocean, the heavens can see through its remotest dept.

OMORE:

And what exactly does that imply?

OMOYE:

My mother once said if a fox is unduly kind toward a chicken, it is because it has a pinch of feeling for it.

OMORE:

Are you assuming I've falling for him or what?

OMOYE:

No! I said no such thing. I think it is natural for all humans to have feelings. Perhaps, I'd rather assume you have a soft spot for him among others.

OMORE:

Heavens know that I make it my business to treat everyone in Udurebo fairly.

OMOYE:

Yes! And that is why Mahke constantly gets into disagreement with you.

OMORE:

Well, that is her headache. I don't flock around species that are not my kind. Our ways are like two parallel lines.

OMOYE:

Hmmm…. Omore (*Pauses*) I fear one thing as I look deep into your eyes.

OMORE:

Fear! (*Looking surprised*) Fear of what?

OMOYE:

My grandfather says when the eyes settle very well it will see the nose. You must beware of wrong feelings, my friend. (*Pauses*) I say this because the after effect could be as bitter as wormwood.

OMORE:

Your riddle confuses me Omoye. Unmask the masquerade for me to see.

OMOYE:

Hmmm… (*She smiles*) You are a princess, while I am just a maid at your service and at the same time your friend. You may detest royalty but your root is your root. The heart of deities may be smooth by the surface yet rough by the edges. Beware my princess, beware. (*She walks away exiting the stage*)

OMORE:

Why does she suddenly become mysteriously proverbial?

(*She turns to face the audience*) Who understands what she speaks? Omoye! Omoye, wait for me! Omoye, I say wait for me! (*She chases after her*)

Exeunt

Act Four Scene One

Enter Itote and Aminebue at a palm wine seller's shop both carrying a jug of calabash. They begin to arrange the stage in readiness for customers.

AMINEBUE:

Mother, have you heard the recent talk in Udurebo about the princess?

ITOTE:

How would I know my daughter when I am rarely present at any of the gossip spots? In my maiden days, I serve the hottest news but now, I have so much in my hands.

AMINEBUE:

Then I take it that you have no interest in the news peddling around?

ITOTE:

Don't get me wrong Aminebue; I never meant I wouldn't like to know.

All I am trying to say is that I now have less time to join the league of gossips. (*Pauses*) So tell me, what evil did they say the princess has committed?

AMINEBUE:
Many say the princess is kind and loving, a few others think she's arrogant.

ITOTE:
Arrogant! Why would anybody think that of her?

AMINEBUE:
Majority of the royal class of Udurebo thinks she is belittling herself, mingling with ordinary citizens.

ITOTE:
You mean it is even the royal class branding her arrogant?

AMINEBUE:
Yes! (*She continue to arrange the stage*)I even heard that she is resolved not to accept a suitor among them.

ITOTE:

Is that possible? I doubt, considering that she is a lone princess. She is bound by tradition to take a husband of a royal root whether within or outside Udurebo.

AMINEBUE:

Rumour has it that she has set her sight on a few men within our land, but yet to make a definite choice among them. Hmm… mother, what makes it more interesting is that suitors from Ogbeani and Ikpena Kingdom not to talk of countless others from our land have visited the king to register their interest.

ITOTE:

Heu! I foresee trouble for our beloved princess, but most of all the man she falls in love with if he's not of royal root. I can only pray that whoever he happens to be should not be related to me.

AMINEBUE:

You sound as if Ememah have pronounced a curse on the princess and her unknown lover, mother.

ITOTE:

Hmmm… my daughter, what an aged woman sees while sitting, a young person cannot see if he or she climbs to the top of Oruku hill. (*Enter four men who take their seats, signaling Itote to come and attend to them*) Good evening, honorable men of our land. You are welcome.

ASEME:

Did she say honorable? Look, woman, you had better be careful with your choice of words else I may be charged for treason.

ITOTE:

Treason! Over what?

ASEME:

Hmmm…one had better beware these days. Men of honor are now jealously guarding their status.

OYASE:

Didn't you hear that every dog, goat, and chicken, is now claiming royalty.

ITOTE:

Why the sudden clamor for royalty?

AGBOTO:

Woman, you speak as if you are a stranger in Udurebo.

ASEME:

All roads lead to the palace. As I speak, there are no spaces for incoming gifts.

OYASE:

Aseme, I am surprised that you are very up to date with this matter. You all know that my late grandfather and the Odafe were good friends.

AGBOTO:

So what about that?

OYASE:

As a favor to the king, I have offered my house for the time being as a haven for gifts coming to His Highness.

So direct all well meaning suitors to my house and then they can go empty handed to see the *Odafe*.

AGBOTO:

If you are not a thief then you must be a dreamer.

OVOAME:

Is any of you aware that even slaves are now claiming royalty?

AGBOTO:

Woman, please bring us some palm wine. I am here to drink and fill my stomach while they do the talking.

ASEME:

I wouldn't blame anybody for all I care. (*He belched*) Have you ever taken time to examine the princess from behind? To be frank, her physical endowments are unmatched in Udurebo.

ITOTE:

Ehnnn… Aminebue! Aminebue!

AMINEBUE:

Yes mother, am all ears.

ITOTE:

Bring our customers some palm wine.

AGBOTO:

I agree with you Aseme. It's obvious that Ememah took a lot of time while forming the princess.

OYASE:

For me, I think Ememah was reallying in good mood before she was formed. It was quite unlike the case of your elder sister, Iretekomo.

AGBOTO:

Look here Oyase; don't start that here or else I'd make you feel the wrath of my fist.

OYASE:

But I was just trying to buttress my point. (*Aminebue brings the palm wine, placing it in front of them*)

AGBOTO:

Then keep on. We shall see if Omokoshe will find it easy identifying you by the time you knock at her hut. (*Ovoame runs his eyes through Aminebue's body as she places drinking bowls of calabash beside the jug of palm wine. Aseme places his hand on her waist but she slaps his hand off her forcefully*)

ASEME:

Ah! That hurts young lady. Is your daughter always that rude to customers?

ITOTE:

Don't you think you've over stepped your boundaries? (*She gave Aseme a bad stare while Agboto shakes the jug of palm wine then pours himself some*)

ASEME:

I was simply being appreciative of the architectural work of nature Ememah bestowed on her.

OVOAME:

I think if placed side by side with the princess your daughter would make some impression too, you know. (*He turns to look at her admiringly and she seems to enjoy it*)

ITOTE:

Thank you for your compliment. (*She walks away, irritated*)

OVOAME:

I do hope the princes of Okpela and Ikpena don't look this way on their way back home. (*Aminebue smiles, enjoying the attention. As Agboto sips his palm wine, Oyase pours himself some, then passes the jug to Aseme*)

OYASE:

The princess as far as I know is not interested in any of those suitors.

AGBOTO:

What makes you so sure of that? Or perhaps you've suddenly become a seer?

OYASE:

I am sure of what I speak.

ASEME:

Yes, I am sure he knows what he's talking about. The sweetness of palm wines is beginning to take toll on his imagination. (*All laugh and sip from their drink*)

OV OAME:

Oyase, did the princess say she will pay her bride price herself? (*All laugh again*) Tell me, have you suffered some malaria bout lately? I ask because I do have a cure for the male type.

OYASE:

Did any of you know that the princess on several occasions paid secret visits to Afeso, the son of the blacksmith, our neighbor? Even yesterday she came under the cover of the night.

AGBOTO:

Really! That I think would make the hottest gossip for the year, especially in the village square.

OVOAME:

Last night I had a strange dream. I saw a young man of our land in shabby clothes whose face I could not recognize, hugging the princess in front of the king.

OYASE:

(*Laughing sarcastically*) Now it's obvious that it was you and not me that is suffering malaria, the male type. And please visit Ogbama the king of mad men; I am sure he'd have a cure for you.

OVOAME:

Emmm… Oyase, when exactly did you lose those two teeth of yours?

OYASE:

Why does it suddenly interest you?

ASEME:

Curiosity I suppose.

OVOAME:

You said since the age of twelve, isn't it? Now I can really see.

OYASE:

What can you see?

OVOAME:

It is because you often open your mouth too wide that Izhedi has not permitted you to have replacement. (*All burst out laughing*)

OYASE:

I thought our elders say wisdom has no price tag; in your case it is foolishness that doesn't.

OVOAME:

To give a blind man a mirror is a mockery of his physical impairment. I blame you not, after all I suddenly realize you lack manners due to your being brought up by an insane mother.

(*Oyase springs to his feet in rage, throwing his palm wine at his face, causing Ovoame to charge towards him but Aseme jumps to his feet to restrain him*)

OYASE:

How dare you raise you filthy mouth against my mother? Look here, the smile of a goat has meaning. Don't dare me because I am a scorpion by the tail.

OVOAME:

Poisonous as a scorpion may be, it is crushed under the mighty feet of an elephant. All you are capable of making is empty threat. I dare you and would dare you more.

OYASE:

(*Laughs sarcastically*) Your challenge excites me my coward friend. The battle line has just been drawn. (*He points at him as Aseme remains in between them*) The next time we meet there will be fire and brimstone. (*He exits*)

ITOTE:

Before you all leave, who pays for the palm wine?

ASEME:

I shall pay for it. (*He dips his hand into his pocket and hands over to her some cowries*) You can keep the excess for all your trouble. (*He turns to Agboto*) You disappoint me Agboto. You sit to drink and wine while you crave blood. I am ashamed of you. (*He exits. Agboto quickly empty his bow of palm wine, chasing after him.*)

Exeunt

Act Four Scene Two

Somewhere in the palace, within the princess quarters. Enter Omore taking her seat, joined by Omoye.

OMORE:

I've been here all by myself, hoping and waiting for you to come and keep me company.(*Her two hands are up ,behind her head, platting herself*)

OMOYE:

I had to attend to the queen. There were some chores she needed me to do for her. Thank god that I am through with them now.

OMORE:

Have you kept Afwone informed about our outing latter in the day?

OMOYE:

I've done just that my princess. (*She pauses to fetch a seat for herself*) Yesterday and the day before, the palace received two important visitors, both with the same mission. It was obvious that His Highness was very pleased with their coming.

OMORE:

Come make my hair for me.(*She drop her hands and then Omoye takes over*) What was so special about these visits that make you think it would interest me?

OMOYE:

They both came with the intent of being a suitor. The princes of Okpela and Ikpena came to register their interest in taking your hand in marriage, my princess. (*She finishes off smiling*)

OMORE:

And why does this very matter excite you? (*She frowns at her*)

OMOYE:

I am not excited but rather worried. Worried because even the king and queen do not understand where your heart lies.

OMORE:

Now that you mentioned it, where do you think my heart lies? (*She rise and begin to pace*)

OMOYE:

I doubt if I can tell, even though it may seem as if I know. The tortoise is a cunning animal, though it claims to know it all yet it knows only little, my princess.

OMORE:

You play cautious my friend. It is because the crocodile knows the worth of its skin that makes it conceal itself under water in vigilance.

OMOYE:

You never seize to amaze me my princess at the dept of your knowledge having to do with life.

Nevertheless, its okay because our elders say a child that washes his hands well will eat with the elders.

OMORE:

(*Comes to sit*)There is a big difference between a cub and a male bear. Mother bear jealously protects its cub but it can never take a bride for adult bear.

OMOYE:

What are you trying to say? That your parents cannot. . .

OMORE:

That I, Omore, the lone princess of Udurebo, have a mind of my own. The turtle dove says that love is not some article that is picked up along the road.

OMOYE:

The princess of Udurebo is young, yet her wisdom dwarfs her youthfulness, still I advice her to look before she leap.

OMORE:

That I'd try not to forget in a hurry. (*Pause*)

After all, a toddler's wisdom is not detachable from its baby sitter.

OMOYE:

One wonders what wisdom a commoner has to impart to royal child.

OMORE:

Much more than you could ever imagine. A humble belly would partake of several dishes.

OMOYE:

When a dog gives birth to a fox, she does not realize its value until it is of age to exhibit the traits of a fox. I do hope the king, head of Udurebo know the rare value of his fox. For certain a chick will become an eagle someday else its not the offspring of an eagle

OMORE:

On the other hand a chick that would grow up to become an eagle must experience several crashes before its wings are strong to keep it afloat in the skies.

OMOYE:

My father says any child that drinks from the tusk of an elephant is destined for greatness. The god of our land have destined you for greatness, but take caution my friend, lest Ememah extinguishes your fire before it is strong enough to burn brightly.

OMORE:

An arrogant baboon will definitely not see the end of the forest. I realize that gray headedness is an asset one dare not throw away.

OMOYE:

The forest existed long beforehand to witness the birth the baboon and must also see its end come what may. Tread softly my friend that you may not offend Ememah that destined you for greatness.

OMORE:

You once said that the tongue that does not roll along carefully with the mouth will end up bitten by the teeth. A wise dog will listen to the whistle of its owner isn't it?

FIRST MAIDEN:
(*Comes in, taking a bow*) My princess, the Queen requests your presence on an urgent matter. (*Bows again and exit*)

OMORE:
Is my hair okay now? (*She rises, looking herself over*) I don't want to keep her waiting.

OMOYE:
You are just okay. (*Wiping some dirt off her*)

OMORE:
Try to get things ready for our outing (*Exit*)

Exeunt

Act Four Scene Three

Somewhere in the forest of Udurebo. Enter Afwone carrying a small bag across his shoulder looking from side to side. Omoye and Omore follow far behind whispering to each other, while Omoye has in her hand a small jug of calabash.

OMOYE:

My princess, we are out of water supply. I'd quickly go down stream to refill our water calabash, if you will permit me.

OMORE:

Please do that very quickly while we wait for your return. (*She exits while Afwone continues to look around*) Afwone!

AFWONE:

(*Approaching her*) Yes my princess!

OMORE:

Come, sit over here beside me and rest while we wait. (*Afwone sits down*)

So tell me, what kingdom do you come from?

AFWONE:

My princess, I'd refer to it as the land of my birth, not my kingdom – the kingdom of Okpetu.

OMORE:

The land of Okpetu. It sounds far away. (*Pause)]* Do you miss this land of your birth as you call it?

AFWONE:

There is nothing to miss about it, except my mother who I may never see again.

OMORE:

Why?

AFWONE:

The monkey says whatever tree the night meets it is its house for the night. My mother conceived me in slavery before her new master brought her to Okpetu. I was born into slavery.

At the moment I am here, without a choice but to get used to whatever I see here.

OMORE:

Hmmm … (*Pauses*) So have you ever liked … I mean loved any woman before?

AFWONE:

Love? (*He shakes his head*) Love is a strange word that should not exist in a slave's world.

OMORE:

Why? After all, they are humans too.

AFWONE:

You've never been in a slave's world and you'd never be. To slaves like me, love is a form of luxury. You are prohibited from falling in love when you don't have freedom.

OMORE:

That is not true. Love is part of life's gift to all.

AFWONE:

You won't understand, my princess.

OMORE:

Make me understand.

AFWONE:

Our world, my princess, are two ways far apart.

OMORE:

Are you trying to say you've never fallen in love before or that you've never felt a strong feeling for someone?

AFWONE:

Your question would stir up my agony were I to answer it.

OMORE:

I'm sorry if it does. In any case, I do need an answer to satisfy my curiosity.

AFWONE:

A slave should stop with admiration, if he must at all. To begin to desire is definitely a disaster. (*Pauses*)

I once fell in love with a fellow slave, but when my master's son discovered this, he made me wait on him while he violated her before my own very eyes! (*Pauses*) My father was a slave but where is he today? I have murdered love, resolving never to admire or desire any woman again whether slave or free born. Of what use is it when one cannot express his feeling freely other than allow it to eat up him till death. (*There was a long pause. Omore rises and begins to pace about*)

OMORE:

Can I ask you a question as a friend?

AFWONE:

A friend! Hmmm. Talking to me the way you've done my princess is an undeserved kindness. Addressing me as a friend is a dream beyond my wildest imaginations.

OMORE:

(*Pauses and paces about*) I am a lone princess of Udurebo kingdom. Shortly, tradition demands of me to choose a groom. A groom of noble birth. For me, choosing a man without loving him is like leprosy. (*Pauses*) Somewhere, hidden away in Udurebo, is a man I know and long for. My heart beats for him. If he can't be mine, my heart will bleed to death without a healing. He is the opposite of nobility, yet I love him more that way. (*She begins to gesture*) I yearn for his touch and warm embrace every night but he doesn't even know it. My eyes are filled with love expression towards him yet he cannot even look me straight in the eyes so as to read them. Someday, the whole world would be up against him by the time it becomes known that I feel strongly for him, but I intend to shield him with my breast and my very life. My hips will be a pillar of support to him and my bosom a haven of shelter. I will protect him jealously the way a lioness protects her cubs. I will go down to my ancestors with the very last drop of my blood, fighting for him. (*Pauses*) I don't know how to tell him how much I yearn to be in his arms, yet I fear his rejection if eventually I summon the courage. I shall not rest until I have his heart in my palms for safe keep. I need to tell him but I do not know how. (*Pauses*) So tell me Afwone, should I tell him or live and die in silence?

AFWONE:

My princess, it is hard to give an advice on a delicate matter that one knows little about, especially in view of the circumstance that may follow. I must also say my inexperience on this matter makes me short of words. (*Pause*) However, if I must advise, then I think it is better to unburden your heart to him, that you may see the end of days. He must choose between ecstasy with death or agony with life. It is his choice to make just as you have made yours. (*Pauses*) In music I find solace, in my flute I unburden my heart. Music is the soul of life; confession is an elixir to the soul. (*She stands looking at Afwone steady in the eyes*)

AFWONE:

Why do you look at me that way my princess? Or have I in any way offended you in my speech?

OMORE:

Oh no! You gave a perfect advice that I intend to implement. (*She walks towards him then goes on her kneels before him*)

AFWONE:

Ah! What are you doing, my princess? (*He jumps to his feet, looking here and there*) Get up please princess! Please get up! I beg of you. (*He tries to help her up but she refuses*)

OMORE:

I would get up only after you have heard me out.

AFWONE:

Okay! Okay! Speak my princess, I am all ears. (*He breathes very fast, looking here and there*) Speak; speak very quickly, my princess.

OMORE:

You are the man of whom I speak! My heart beats for you, Afwone. It weighs me down so much that I can no longer keep it within me.

AFWONE:

Heu!   Heuuuu…
Heuuuuu….Heuuuuuuuuuu…. (*He moans and begins to flee from her*)
Heuuuuu…!Heuuuuuu..!Heuuuuu!
Ugbemeyaooo… Ugbemeyaooo…
You've killed me…You've killed me
Ugbemeyaooo…Ugbemeyaooo…
You've killed me…You've killed me
Ugbemeyaooo… Ugbemeyaooo…
You've killed me…You've killed me
(*He continues to moan until he exits. Enters Omoye with a jug of water   and meets her kneeling down*)

OMOYE:

What happened, my princess? Tell me Omore. I saw Afwone running and weeping. (*She drops the jug and helps her up, rising to her feet*)

OMORE:

I told him the truth. (*Pauses*) He is scared of love. He has murdered love in his heart. (*She breaks out crying*) He will never love me. He said he would never love any woman again. Not even me.

OMOYE:

Omore! Omore!

OMORE:

(*Crying*) He said he would never love any woman again, including me.

OMOYE:

Omore, look at me.(*She held her by the shoulder*) He is already in love with you.

OMORE:

How do you know? He just told me that he can never love any woman again.

OMOYE:

I know he is in love with you long ago because his eyes constantly tell me so. Get a grip of yourself and leave the rest to me.

Exeunt

Act Four Scene Four

Stage opens behind the palace, somewhere at the slave's quarters with a poorly-lit stage. Afwone comes on to lay a mat and goes to sleep. Omoye comes in carrying a burning lamp. She taps him by the feet to wake him up

OMOYE:
Wake up, wake up Afwone!

AFWONE:
Who is it? (*He sits up*)

OMOYE:
Shee! It is me Omoye, keep your voice down.

AFWONE:
What do you want from me at this hour of the night?

OMOYE:
Why did you have to provoke the princess so much to tears?

She has been weeping ever since.

AFWONE:

And how does her crying got anything to do with me?

OMOYE:

Don't pretend as if you do not know. Do you realize how serious it is for her to weep?

AFWONE:

May be you should tell me.(*Rise to his feet*)

OMOYE:

The queen is worried. The gods forbid her from crying. If it is prolonged, the land of Udurebo would be doomed. She said Omore must stop crying before it is too late.

AFWONE:

Is it not enough trouble being a slave? So why must she ask of me what is not in my power to give?

OMOYE:

Was it too much for her to express her genuine feeling toward you?

AFWONE:

She might as well put an axe to my head and chop it off.

OMOYE:

It seems to me that what she is offering you is a life-time opportunity. You could be a free man for once in your life.

AFWONE:

No; what she is offering me is a quick way to death!(*Gesturing*)

OMOYE:

Are you saying all she said to you this evening in the forest does not mean anything to you?

AFWONE:

Look Omoye, I am a slave and I've been there before. It is easy being a free born than a slave such as I am.

Life is in black and white. For a slave love is only one side: life or death. I want to choose life with all its burdens.

OMOYE:

But who knows, life is full of changes. This is an opportunity to be a king and be free.

AFWONE:

Slaves don't dream such dreams, Omoye. Keep day dreaming for as long as you want but I shall not be part of it.

OMOYE:

Nothing is impossible in this world we live in.

AFWONE:

One thing that is constant in the life of a slave is humiliation and untimely death.

OMOYE:

Even if you won't bulge to the princess' proposal, think of Udurebo.

AFWONE:

You amaze me. The land of my birth didn't even think before I was sold, how much more Udurebo that I barely know.

OMOYE:

Are you now telling me you don't wish for freedom?

AFWONE:

If wishes were horses beggars would be able to ride on them Omoye.

OMOYE:

You leave me no choice but to tell the queen that you are the cause of her daughter's weeping?

AFWONE:

(*Claps both hands*)Please do that very quickly and don't forget to tell her also that you gave consent to her falling in love with a slave instead of nobles. Threats don't move me Omoye. I have very little to loose, considering the fact that I am a slave.

OMOYE:

(*She pauses to look at him in confusion*) What kind of man are you? I wonder if you were really worth all the attention Omore invested in you. Love, they say, is like a rolling blind stone down the hill. Well, I'd tell the princess that you said all she said in the forest does not mean anything to you right away.

AFWONE:

Ah! You would say no such thing to her Omoye. (*Almost jumping at her*)

OMOYE:

(*She pause in thought*) Hmmm.... I suddenly get his attention. Imagine! It surprises me that Princess Omore of all people weeps over a mere slave and his head is getting swollen at that.

AFWONE:

(*Humbly*) Okay, tell her that I'd give a thought to her proposal.

OMOYE:

(*Pause in thought*) Thankgod that he is now becoming more reasonable. All I do is for her and our friendship.

AFWONE:

I'd remind you of all you said if it ever happens. But never forget I refuse to believe it.

OMOYE:

Ah! You are too negative for my liking. (*She makes to exit*)

AFWONE:

Greet the princess for me; I wish her a pleasant night rest. (*She ignores him*)

Exeunt

Act Five Scene One

In the king's vineyard, enter Omore looking around, then takes a seat. After a while Afwone comes on looking here and there in search. Omore comes from behind and jumps at him.

AFWONE:

Ah! You really scare me, Omore.

OMORE:

Yes, I wanted to scare you for the fact that you kept me waiting for so long.

AFWONE:

Slaves don't make plans, their masters do, don't forget that.

OMORE:

Must you constantly remind me that you are a slave?

AFWONE:

As often as you remember that, the longer you'd help keep me alive.

OMORE:

I hate it when time and again you stress death as the end result of our relationship.

AFWONE:

Okay, I'm sorry if my words annoy you. However, such frank views help me to deal with facts rather than get emotional with issues. A spade should be called by its name.

OMORE:

So why did you keep me waiting in this lonely vineyard?

AFWONE:

Your father demanded my service to entertain his guest. Or does a slave have an objection against his master's wish? Hmmm. The day he does is the day he stops appreciating life.

OMORE:

Your manly view of life with logical reason to delicate matter is what interests me the most about you. I think I am most fortunate to be loved by you.(*She picks his hair*)

AFWONE:

Your overwhelming beauty glows brilliantly like a star in a night sky. (*She sits to enjoy his poetic utterances*) Your breasts are like precious gold longed for by every man and your curved hips like pillars of diamond. Your eyes balls are pearls of rare value that allures me each day. The warm embrace you give puts me on a mountain of ecstasy. The smile on your face casts an irresistible spell on me. Pain would come and go, tribulation definitely would hurt me later, but the love you give I am taking with me for eternity. Death is an enemy, but with your love I shall conquer the cruelty of humanity. I have secured an abode amidst serenity and peaceful delight fondling my soul. Death is pain, death is loss but death in love is a rare experience beyond imagination. I have won love, I've won a heart, and I've received a crown with a princess. I have shed tears, I'd feel pains but eventually my death shall tell a story that has never been told. Slavery is agony, why nobility is pride of honor but with your affection I am redefining life. Slave I may be but I am a noble at heart, yes a noble of love. I am invisibly untouchable. You could humiliate and strip me of dignity but no one can tear my heart from passion because I have won love on a pedestal.

OMORE:

Afwone, you are a slave yet you speak with the heart of a noble.

AFWONE:

True I was born a slave but my master raised me as a son. If I speak like a noble it is because I am a noble slave.(*He find a seat for himself close to her*)

OMORE:

If really this your master loved you that much why didn't he set you free?

AFWONE:

Were it not for sudden death he would have set me free as he promised. I think Ememah never destined me for freedom.(*Rise and walk away*)

OMORE:

Why do you speak that way?(*Rise approaching him*)

AFWONE:

My master's two sons hated me because their father treated me as a special slave. He once said I was a son he never had to his sons and that provoked their anger the more toward me. So when my master died, they vented their rage on me, eventually they sold me. In some ways I was happy but for my mother I was sad because I may never see her again.

OMORE:

Oh I am sorry. I share your sadness (*She embrace him consolingly. While they hug Igbe enters. He clears his throat to register his presence causing them to quickly disengage*)

IGBE:

Sorry for interrupting my princess. I do not mean to pry.

OMORE:

What are you doing here then?

IGBE:

(*Peeping at Afwone who tries to hide behind Omore*)

I have the privilege of caring for His Majesty's vineyard this week my princess.

OMORE:

I am sure you did not see anything when you came here, or did you?

IGBE:

Ehmm…yes, I mean my princess, I saw nothing.(*Swinging his hands back and forth*)

OMORE:

That is good. You saw nothing and you must say nothing.

IGBE:

Yes my princess. I must attend to my duties at once. (*As he was about to start attending to his duties, Omore calls him*)

OMORE:

Igbe

IGBE:

Yes, my princess.

OMORE:

Send your daughter, Aminebue, to me this evening. I think I have something that would interest you.

IGBE:

Ah! Thank you very much my princess. May the god bless your generosity. (*Afwone quickly hurries away*)

OMORE:
It is nothing to thank me for. (*She exits*)

Exeunt

Act Five Scene Two

In the palace, enter Eremase along with chiefs taking their seats. Two royal guards stand on both sides of the king.

EREMASE:

I have called you all to know how the various arrangements delegated to you are going. You know tomorrow is the big day when my daughter would eventually choose her groom. It is needless to mention how important this fortunate man would be.

THIRD CHIEF:

(*He rises to gesture in explanation, pacing*)Most certainly, Your Highness. I have personally arranged for plenty of drinks – palm wine. The best tappers have all been duly contacted. They've all reassured me that they would start bringing them in from this very evening.

EREMASE:

That is good. I trust you won't fail me. And what about you, how far have you gone?

SECOND CHIEF:

(*Rises and clearing his throat*)Your Majesty, all the hunters in Udurebo have been made to realize the importance of tomorrow.(*Pacing now*) In fact, since yesterday lots of bush meat have been coming in to the palace. Many more are on the way. Two large cows have just arrived.(*Pointing toward back of the palace*) All the clans in Udurebo have given five goats each to support the occasion along with food items. The market women have flooded the palace premises with yam tuber and several others food items. (*Gesturing*) My eagerness now is for tomorrow to come. (*Return to sit*)

EREMASE:

True, there is hardly any space left here in the palace for gift items. Well done. It is important everyone be well fed.

My only child, the lone princess of Udurebo, must not just be given out as an ordinary woman in Udurebo. (*He turns to face first chief*) It's time to hear from you.

FIRST CHIEF:

(*Rises and bow*)I have arranged for great musicians from the land of Ereden and Ogori to thrill the audience.(*Looks from side to side*) Even our local musicians would all be handy to keep the spirit of the occasion alive. However one area we cannot over look is security. Our warriors would be on the alert at strategic locations in case our enemies decide to take us by surprise even though I am sure they would not dare.

EREMASE:

(*Nodding approval, waving his staff*) That is very thoughtful of you. When a man looks back and sees a crowd behind him, he feels bold to speak to enemies at the gate. I must commend you all, for you've done well. Our people say there is no prestige for a king who has no queen.

Ignoring the fact that my daughter is of age is like pretending that one does not need a heir to carry on his name.

FIRST CHIEF:

That is very true your highness. (*Rises but remain still*)When a male chick is of age one does not need special rituals before pronouncing it a cock. Come tomorrow Omore would choose her groom before the King and Queen of Udurebo.

SECOND CHIEF:

(*Rises to bow*) But your highness, there are some rumors peddling around Udurebo.

FIRST CHIEF:

(*Still standing*) Rumors! You mean you of all people pay attention to gossip?

SECOND CHIEF:

(*Ignores him*) My late uncle use to say that every rumor or gossip peddling around have its own fair share of truth.

THIRD CHIEF:

That is very true Your Highness.(*Also rise to join others*) To get hold of the truth one must learn to pay attention to every little gossip no matter what their intentions are.

EREMASE:

So what rumor have you heard?

SECOND CHIEF:

(*Clears his throat and pause*) I heard the princess said she is not interested in any of the suitors that have been coming to ask for her hand.

THIRD CHIEF:

I even heard too that she said she would not take any husband among the nobles

SECOND CHIEF:

(*Cuts in*) Some one went as far as saying that she said she would rather choose a groom among slaves than nobles.

THIRD CHIEF:
That even as we speak she has chosen her groom. I could choose to be silent over this matter but our people say a stitch in time saves nine.

EREMASE:
Have you finished?

SECOND CHIEF:
Ah yes.(*Second and third chief sit*)

THIRD CHIEF:
We've finished Your Highness.

EREMASE:
(*Pause for a while*) It is a shame when men of honor throw away honor to embrace stupidity. You mean while you should have been busy deliberating on matters about the kingdom you were instead gossiping about in Udurebo. If I have heard this from other sources it would have been less painful. (*Pauses*) You even had nothing to gossip about but my innocent daughter.

Is it not a shame? It is a shame when the camel gulps down the excrement of a dog. I thought I knew my chiefs well. I now know better that they are women by the mouth but men by chest. Were it not for the fact that you are my chiefs I would have confined you to the dungeon until after tomorrow. (*Pauses*) Since it is clear that you don't have better things to say, I'd retire to my inner chambers (*Exits Eremase and then followed by first chief. Second and third chief remain, whispering and gesturing to each other. They rise to exit*)

Exeunt

Act Five Scene Three

Enter King Eremase, Queen Amume followed by two body guards, chiefs and three elders sitting. Noble suitors numbering into seven come in to join them greeting all before sitting down. Townspeople's voices are heard and then fade into the background. Suddenly musical instrument begin to play with melodic rhythm. Group of female dancers enter from the right, dancing to thrill the audience and then exit through the left. Acrobats come on to perform and then exit. Musical instrument continue to play for a while before gradually fading away.

FIRST ELDER:

(Rises to consult king before speaking) People of Udurebo I greet you. *(His voice is drowned by townspeople's voices causing him to pause)* I greet you all, even our visitors from neighboring kingdoms. You are all welcome once again to this grand occasion.

Out of His Majesty's and his Queen's generosity we have all dined and wined in merriment. This is because their only daughter who has come of age today will take up a groom from among our honorable suitors here. (*Pause*) Today is a day every parent eagerly looks forward to for their daughter. The toad said it does not believe in procrastination that is why it cuts off its tail. It is now time for our princess to come and show us who the favored one is among her suitors. Once again I greet you people of Udurebo and our honorable visitors.

(Townspeople's voices fill the air, as princess comes on stage escorted by maidens. Townspeople's voices are up again then fade. A steward hands over a cup of calabash filled with palm wine to first Elder)

Omore, our daughter, the lone princess of Udurebo, we welcome you. The whole of our people are gathered here today because of you.

Today is a day you must choose, telling us who among these noble men will be your husband. Take this from me and hand it over to the very one among them. (*She receives it with both hands and begins to go around in search among the crowd. All the men, young and old on stage, stretch their hand to her, as voice of townspeople fills the air. After going round, she pause and face the crowd then begins to drink from the cup of calabash in her hand until it is empty, dropping it on the ground. Townspeople's voice gets louder, all in surprise*)

TOWNSPEOPLE:

Ah! Ah what is she doing? Ah this is an abomination

Ah, nothing of this has happened before in Udurebo (*The murmuring voices of townspeople rise. All in the palace is shocked at her action*)

FIRST ELDER:

(*Looks confuse*) Our dear princess, (*Pause*) what you have just done is unheard of in our land. Please tell us, what does this action of yours mean?

(Townspeople's voice remain in the background)

OMORE:

The very man that drinks from the cup on my hand eventually becomes my chosen husband, isn't it?

FIRST ELDER:

You are very right my daughter.

OMORE:

(She turns to address the audience gesturing) My action may fail all here especially His Majesty the king. But think of it, how do I marry a man without loving him? Among all these suitors the man I love is not found. The one I love is out there, looked down by many and despised by all. I yearn for him and only him.*(Pause)* Doesn't what a young maiden feel and want matter? I have chosen a wise man not necessarily of noble birth but noble in his own world. I shall love him even down to death.

I Omore shall not be a gift item that any man can pick up along the way for his own selfish ambition of coveting the throne of Udurebo. The throne of Udurebo is pure and sacred. When a man covets the throne with ulterior motive, his heart becomes corrupt and crooked. Purity becomes alien to his body and soul.(*Pause*) Deep down inside me, I feel as if I do not belong here. Why, because my words are strange and irritating especially to those of noble birth. Why must some men play the gods and Lord over others when all humans are born equal? (*The suitors rise and begin to exit one after the other, taking a bow as murmurings of townspeople's fill the air followed by the elders'*)

AMUME:

(*Queen comes on stage*)My daughter, why have you decided to shame your father and I? All we've done is what is best for you.

OMORE:

What you think is best for me, mother, is not good enough for me. (*Townspeople exit, remaining king elders and chiefs*)

EREMASE:

Were you not my only child I would have disowned you as a bastard. Get out of my sight before I am tempted to do what I'd later regret! (*Shouting as she exits, running off stage followed by her mother. Second and third chief whisper in low tone, gesturing*) Aah! It makes more sense to me now. Every rumor peddling around has its own fair share of truth. It is wise to pay attention to the parrots despite being a talkative. I have shamed my chiefs, I have insulted their loyalty, I have shamed my crown. (*He rises to his feet*)

SECOND CHIEF:

But Your Majesty, it is. . .

EREMASE:

Say nothing more. Say nothing more. Let the honored eat shame, let the crown eat pride.

(*He turns to face first chief*) You must find me this man who has instigated my daughter against me. That he shames me, he shames his head. That he made me a laughing stock, his body I shall feed the vultures. (*He speaks with rage*) His eye balls I shall feed to the eagles. So find him! Find him! Find him! (*He exits and first chief and elders goes after him*)

THIRD CHIEF:

That one wears the crown does not mean he has acquired all wisdom.

SECOND CHIEF:

If only he had listened, perhaps this could have been averted.

THIRD CHIEF:

When the crown becomes power drunk it completely loses all sense of reasoning. (*They both exit*)

Exeunt

Act Five Scene Four

Somewhere behind the palace, enter Afwone with a piece of firewood and an axe trying to split it. Omore enters in sober mood.

AFWONE:
What are you doing here when you are supposed to be getting married?

OMORE:
What sort of talk is that? Are you saying you are happy I am getting married?

AFWONE:
Not really, but, it does seem wise to me you should be married to a groom that truly suites you: A noble man who would make a good king and as well accord you dignity.

OMORE:
Well I have just disappointed you.

I rejected all those that came with a hope. I told Udurebo I'm in love and have made my choice.

AFWONE:

Ehuu! (*Drop axe and walk away from her*)Omore, you will kill me sooner than I had ever thought by this daring action of yours.

OMORE:

Are you also asking me to marry a man I have no love for, Afwone? I thought you promised to love me till the end of times?

AFWONE:

I will never deny that. I will love you till death. But don't forget that Igbe already know things about us, and it will spread faster than you can know. The odds will be against me.

OMORE:

No one dare touches you, my love.(*She walk toward him, placing her hand on his shoulder from behind*) If you bleed once, I bleed twice.

AFWONE:

I understand that your heart is strong for love but you are too young to comprehend this thing. (*Walks away further*)For a slave to be in love with a princess is a crime against Udurebo. All eyes will be against us.

OMORE:

For the first time since my birth I saw rage in the eyes of my father toward me. As we speak, he is threatening to disown me. I am not afraid to speak the truth. I shall be queen but I need a king that is uncorrupted by sentimental nobility.

AFWONE :

(*Turning to face her*) Omore you are starting a fight you can never win. Your fight is against Udurebo, not one man. At the end of it all the buck ends up at my door post – the very victim of their rage. By your action today, you have just sentenced me to death.

OMORE:

No! Don't say that. (*She moves close to hug him*) You cause me much pain when you speak that way. If you cry, I'd bleed; your agony is my death. Your death means my funeral.

AFWONE:

Omore, I feel privileged to be loved by you but the agony that awaits me is what I fear the most.

OMORE:

Speak no further please, my love, or else I'd die of mental torment inflicted on me by your words. (*The queen walks into them causing Afwone to quickly disengage from her*)

AMUME:

Ah! (*Clapping her hands in surprise*) What are you doing with my daughter? You were planning to rape her right under my nose, here in the palace? So you are the one feeding my child with lies, instigating her against her own father?

You have brainwashed her by bewitching her. Ehuu! I wish I had believed Igbe's words. A slave manipulating the princess for your own selfish sexual lust?

OMORE:

No, mother, he did not such thing. Never, ever!

AMUME:

Come! Come, come my child. I hope he has not succeeded in gaining entrance into the orchard? (*She pulls her by the hand away from him, and rains several slaps on him*)

OMORE:

No, no no! Stop it mother! If you raise up your hand against him once more I shall bleed. (*She picks up a knife on the floor*)

AMUME:

A slave fondling my own daughter, the princess of Udurebo! (*She picks up a stick and strikes him with it*)

AFWONE:

Aaaah! Aaaah! Aaaah! (*Fall to the floor. He flees from her, crawling*)

OMORE:

Mother! I warned you mother but you ignore me, now you will pay. (*She cuts herself with the knife*) Aah! Aaah!

AMUME:

Aaah! My child, you are bleeding. This slave has killed me. Blood, blood my child (*Maids and body guards rush in. She holds her bleeding hand but Omore flees from her*)

OMORE:

I shall do that even more each time you try to hurt him. (*Afwone runs, bodyguard chases after him*)

AMUME:

Okay, I shall hurt him no more. Please just hand me the knife and allow me attend to your wound. (*She drops the knife while Amume holds her by the hand. They exit, followed by maids*)

Nathaniel Apheyso

Exeunt

...

Act Five Scene Five

In the palace, enter Eremase, chiefs and elders sitting. Two bodyguards bring in Afwone with his hand tied behind him.

EREMASE:

Ah there he is, the slave I bought with my own money, yet shames me in public. You are the one that instigate my own child against me. You shall regret this, you'd pay dearly.

SECOND CHIEF:

Young man, is it true you instigated the princess against the king? (*No answer*) Answer me or are you deaf?

THIRD CHIEF:

The adventurous wolf has suddenly lost its taste for blood. May be he has suddenly become dumb.

FIRST ELDER:

Tell us, young man, the very truth of the matter. Was it you that pressured the princess into this illicit relationship or did she seduce you?

AFWONE:

Your Majesty, though I am a slave, still I am contented with being one. I shall never take side with your enemies against you My Lord.

FIRST CHIEF:

Traitors plot and scheme evil, yet it is their finger that they have burnt in the end. The very evil you scheme shall consume you to the dust.

SECOND ELDER:

Tell me, they say you raped the princess right here inside the palace.

AFWONE:

May Ememah strike me dead this instant were it true, Old One.

SECOND CHIEF:

That would imply that the queen lied then, isn't it? (*He refuses to reply*) Answer me!(*Shouting*)

AFWONE:

I'd dare not say she lied. It's better to say she painted the matter in bold colors.

THIRD CHIEF:

What is it in particular that she painted bold?

AFWONE:

Actually the princess…she…she was hugging me, holding on tightly to me when the queen met us.

THIRD ELDER:

You mean the princess hugged you, not you hugging her?

AFWONE:

God knows I speak the truth.

THIRD ELDER:

Did it not occur to you that hugging the princess as a slave is the same thing as raping her?

AFWONE:

The princess, she….she just won't take "no" for an answer.

FIRST CHIEF:

But you enjoyed her advances and craved the excitement, didn't you? You dreamed of freedom and perhaps…

AFWONE:

No! That's not true. She stubbornly held on tight, not willing to let go.

SECOND CHIEF:

Watch your tongue slave. You dare to insult the king's daughter in front of His Majesty?

AFWONE:

I am sorry Your Highness.

SECOND ELDER:

You bewitched her with your evil spells,
did you not?

AFWONE:

I did no such thing, Old One.

SECOND ELDER:

Then how come she made well her threat,
almost slaying herself? She bled herself to
rescue you from the queen's wrath,
enabling you to flee.

AFWONE:

It is the strangest thing anyone could ever
do. I didn't understand what she was
thinking to have done that.

THIRD CHIEF:

In her rage she did it for you a mere slave.
The princess shed her blood for you
instead of you doing otherwise.

AFWONE:

I would do same for her if our
circumstance were to be in the reverse
side.

THIRD CHIEF:

Aha! You just said it. You were in love with her, were you not? Speak the truth and let the gods bear you witness.

AFWONE:

I must admit, we felt strongly for each other. Yes, I did love her and I'd continue to love her even in death. I knew all along that to be in love with her would be treason and now the whole world is up against me.

FIRST CHIEF:

You were in love with her, so you manipulated her, instigating her against her father and people. You bewitched her causing her to lose all sense of reasoning. She bled for a mere slave due to your evil spells making her resent our culture and tradition.

SECOND CHIEF:

You are evil, filled with evil intent. The evil which you seek for others shall definitely come upon you.

THIRD CHIEF:

You are guilty and you said it yourself. You shame this very council in the glare of the public, trampling down our tradition.

THIRD ELDER:

This very deed of yours is a crime in our land, a crime against Udurebo.

FIRST ELDER:

We shall charge you of treason against the land of Udurebo. Slaves don't fall in love with the citizen, yet you did the worst by falling in love with the lone princess of our kingdom.

SECOND ELDER:

The king who you despise and shame will now pronounce judgment on you. (*There is a pause*)

EREMASE:

(*He clears his throat*) I, Eremase, king of Udurebo, hereby pronounce judgment of execution on you by an axe that your case may serve as a detterrent to others.

ALL IN PALACE:

Iseeeeh! (*There was black out, followed by sorrowful humming for a while. The voice of Omore is heard on the dark stage*)

OMORE:

No! No! No! Nooooooo! Nooooooo! Nooooooo! ….No, no, no, no, noooo… Aaah! Aaaaah! Aaaaaah! (*She cried for a while before speaking*) Aah! Mother land, land of Udurebo why do you spite me? (*Crying*) Udurebo, you shall feel my rage. But when you do, you must not cut me. Because when you cut me I shall bleed. And when I bleed I will die. But before I die, I shall curse you. And when I curse you, you will burn. If you burn, Udurebo will come to ashes. When she comes to ashes, she will mourn. And her mourning shall ascend for eternity. (*Humming of dirge fills the dark stage along with gong and metallic beating while Omore continues to cry.*

Sounds gradually fade away. Stage lit up every now and then with night noise. Healer comes on stage to address the audience with bunch of leaves in hand. She examines them, and then looks up before speaking)

HEALERS:

King Eremase imposed a chosen husband on her daughter after the execution of Afwone. At least that was what he taught was right. Hmmm… for Omore, she mourned her lover for ninety days and there after paid Udurebo back in her own deed. (*Pauses*) She slew her chosen husband, and then took her own life. (*Pauses*) The king of Udurebo ignored the warning not to provoke his child's anger, allowing her to have whatever she wanted. Perhaps he fail to realize that choosing who so ever she wanted to love was part of the deal and so paid with the loss of everything, his only child- the future of Udurebo, all because of pride. Though one must admit that king Eremase was pitched between the devil and the deep blue sea. That was what happened many years ago in the land of Udurebo. (*Pauses*) Love is crazy, strange and unpredictable don't you think? It always makes an interesting subject to both young and old alike.(*Pause*)But look back critically. Have we learnt anything? Rich or poor, you must learn never to trade your child's heart for prestige, fame or wealth, because non worth their life. The king of Egbetua, Ogbaji was about making the same mistake Eremase made but was advised otherwise. Would he listen or allow pride and prestige make him hold a stone heart?(*Pause*) He left that night being indecisive as to what was paramount. In any case, he must bear his burden alone. Am sure he knows where to find me if eventually he comes around to see reasons for a change of heart. We can only hope it wouldn't have been too late then.

(As she exit, there are flashes of light every now and then on the dark stage accompanied by beating of musical instrument, along with humming in the background, all in sorrowful manner. Beating gradually fades into the back ground)

Curtain Falls

ABOUT THE AUTHOR

www.ingramcontent.com/pod-product-compliance
Lightning Source LLC
Chambersburg PA
CBHW020929160726
47993CB00005B/2194